Celestine Sibley

CELESTINE SIBLEY

MOTHERS Are Always SPECIAL

Illustrations by Scarlett B. Rickenbaker

PEACHTREE PUBLISHERS, LTD.

Published by
PEACHTREE PUBLISHERS, LTD.
494 Armour Circle, N.E.
Atlanta, Georgia 30324

Manufactured in the United States of America

ISBN: 0-931948-73-8

To Muv, of course

MOTHERS Are Always SPECIAL

Chapter 1

UNTIL RECENT YEARS my mother, Muv, regarded Mother's Day as a big fat joke perpetrated on an acquiescent populace by the gift and greeting card industry. Long before Philip Wylie's tirade against "momism" in the 1940s Muv thought Saintly Silver-haired Mother was mostly a myth and that mothers, far from being stronger, wiser and better than real people, were often saboteurs boring from within to weaken and undermine the spines, minds and emotions of their sons and daughters.

Orphaned early herself, she knew enough about other people's mothers to hold them suspect. A mother, she conceded, was a biological necessity. But after she had birthed and suckled her young the relationship deteriorated rapidly. It seemed perfectly plausible to her that Tarzan (played by Johnny Weissmuller in those days) might have been reared by apes to be a fine upstanding young man.

The only trouble, she mused, looking distractedly at

her own young swinging on the topmost branch of the chinquapin tree in the yard in south Alabama, was that apes were in short supply in this country.

By contrast, Muv's child and later her grandchildren celebrated Mother's Day with energy, ardor and dusting powder. We made her loving-hands-at-home gifts, torturing unresisting cloth with cross-stitch and French knots. We painted her pictures — crayoned pansies and livid watercolor roses. We memorized terrible poems. ("I love you, Mother," said little Nell. "I love you more than tongue can tell.") And we sang — relentlessly — songs about "Mother o'Mine," although there wasn't a drop of Irish blood in either side of the family, and that unabashed acrostic beginning, "M is for the million things . . ."

Muv, caught between embarrassment and an unaccountable rush of tenderness for us, sometimes got a little teary over these demonstrations but more often she would cross her eyes clownishly, cut a wild buck and wing and make satirical remarks about "deah old mothaw."

That was until recently.

Now Muv lives in a little northwest Florida town where the population runs heavily to elderly widows and there isn't much to do between church socials and Lawrence Welk but gather at the post office and play one-upmanship with the morning mail.

Essie's daughter, Voncile, writing from Newark twice a week doesn't shine half so brightly as Maude's Latitia, who sends thirty-five-cent satin heart cards with sachet hidden inside on Valentine's Day and celebrates Mother's Day with nylon nightgowns and peignoirs to be stored away against some unforeseen, calamitous trip to the hospital.

It's not the gift that counts, of course. (Not a one of them is like the forthright old lady we know who shakes the cards and notes from her far-flung clan and, if nothing falls out, drops them, unread, into the trash basket with a dirty word.) It's just that a nice, expensive gift is unmistakable evidence of thought. And a lot of gifts . . . well, you get the idea.

This would seem to bear out Bishop G. Bromley Oxnam's theory that when it comes to mothers the child is the proof of the pudding. Good mother: devoted child. Great mother: distinguished child.

The Methodist bishop in his celebrated Mother's Day sermon, "Behold Thy Mother," reported that on the back of the portrait of Whistler's Mother there's a portrait of a child. It may have been that Whistler had just run out of canvas when he started his famous "Arrangement in Grey and Black" but Bishop Oxnam read another meaning into it.

It was as it should be, he said. "There can be no painting of a mother without the face of a child upon the other side of the canvas. . . . All great mothers have been created by their sons and daughters. No matter how intrinsically great a mother may have been, history accords her no such recognition if the son or daughter fail her. Who would have heard of Mary, the Madonna, if Jesus of Nazareth failed her? . . . Who was the mother of Judas? No one knows."

It seems to me that the bishop put undue strain on both mother and child, overlooking the part that genes, the times, destiny, papa and even the kids down

3

the block might play in shaping a life. Nancy Hanks might never have had race horses named for her or, in Atlanta, a train, if Abraham Lincoln hadn't made it beyond clerking in a country store, but her job of work as a mother would have been the same.

Come to think of it, who knows for sure how good a mother Nancy really was? She died when Abe was young and the most we have is his word that she was a wonderful woman. This is, of course, prejudiced testimony. Most children love their mothers. As "Jimmie" Whistler is reported to have said of the portrait of his maternal parent: "One does like to make one's mummy just as nice as possible."

The truth is fame and fortune call only a fraction of the sons and daughters of the world. Success in child rearing and, it follows, in motherhood is relative. Rearing a prophet or a president is success for one mother. Keeping a house full of children from starving to death or out of jail is the ultimate in achievement for another.

It had to be the unsung mothers the Congress and President Woodrow Wilson had in mind on May 8, 1914, when they passed a joint resolution and issued a proclamation calling for displaying the flag on government buildings and private homes "as a public expression of our love and reverence for the mothers of our country."

Since 1908, when Miss Anna Jarvis got the thing started in Philadelphia, somebody — probably women, *mother*-type women — had been nagging Congressmen and Presidents to do something about a national Mother's Day. They spoke in those days in florid terms of mother's "sweetness, purity and endurance," likening her to the white carnation, which became her floral emblem. Women didn't give birth. They "went down into the valley of the shadow of death." And the mortality rate for both mothers and infants being what it was, it was no euphemism.

A Presbyterian church in Seattle took up the cause and by 1910 all the churches in Seattle were setting aside a Sunday service to honor motherhood. The word was to bring Mama to church or write her a letter if she lived and to wear a white carnation if she was dead. Women members came into the church with bouquets of flowers and on a given signal from the pulpit they all stood up, waving their posies aloft, later taking them out to decorate the graves of dead mothers.

It followed that the very next Presbyterian President, Woodrow Wilson, backed by Congressional action, would proclaim the second Sunday in May as a time to honor "the American mother . . . the greatest source of this country's strength and inspiration, the American Mother, who is doing so much for the home, for moral uplift and religion, hence so much for good government and humanity."

It wasn't exactly what the politicians call a Mother Hubbard type accolade, covering everything, touching nothing, but it came close. It said nothing about the countless non-mothers who were and still are doing a mother's job — stepmothers, grandmothers, foster mothers, spinster schoolteachers who skimp along to educate nieces and nephews, plain, lumpish, uninspired women who didn't think much about gov-

5

ernment and humanity but who did the best they could where they stood to bring up somebody else's children.

Around the newspaper where I work, old-timers can always get a laugh from one another on glum days by calling out when they meet in the hall: *"Where are you, Mrs. Fannie Lou Ledbetter?"*

One Monday morning years ago we opened our newspaper to find the lead on a page-one story. "Where are you, Mrs. Fannie Lou Ledbetter?" asked the first paragraph, and even if most of us hadn't known who Mrs. Fannie Lou Ledbetter was and how long she had been missing, there was still something about it — the name, the lilting quality of the question — that caused us to howl in merriment.

Actually, it wasn't funny. Mrs. Fannie Lou Ledbetter was a mother, a young mother, and obviously not one President Wilson would have set up for national veneration. She had walked out on her three children one day. When last seen she was hopping nimbly into a truck on U. S. Highway 29, headed south.

Her old mother was stuck with the children, no money, the rent past due, the groceries gone and Mr. Ledbetter, if there was one, nowhere in sight either. Somehow the old lady muddled through, making periodic trips to police headquarters and to the newspaper to ask if there was any word from the missing Fannie Lou.

We ran her picture, the police broadcast her description, with no result. After she had been missing for months her eldest child, a little boy, was found to be losing his eyesight and the poor grandmother frantically got to work marshaling the city's medical and charitable resources to get him the necessary operation.

She made one final visit to the newspaper to sound a plea for the child's mother to come home. A young reporter, caught up in the thing and, it being Sunday night, the city editor's hand not there to restrain him, let fire with that question: "Where are you, Mrs. Fannie Lou Ledbetter?"

As far as I know it was never answered. The child had the operation and recovered. The grandmother, bless her, to this day may consider herself a failure because of her recalcitrant daughter.

But to those of us who observed her struggle to rear the missing Fannie Lou's children she appeared to be a splendid mother. Not exactly fun-loving, it's true. She once confided that the thing that probably caused Fannie Lou to leave home in the first place was her refusal to let her buy a motorcycle with the rent money the last time they had some.

But she did a mother's job under adverse circumstances and there are many like her. Not radiant madonnas, not silver-haired saints but ordinary women, stumbling along with neither special knowhow nor a special vision, rearing children as well as they can. Some of them aren't exactly carnations, notable for their sweetness and purity, but nearly all of them have had their lives illumined at least for a time by active, working, mountain-moving love.

This book is about some of these very special mothers.

Chapter 2

ALL MOTHERS — ALL people, I suppose — reach a point some time in life when they feel unequal to the task they've tackled and are assailed by doubt and fear. Most of us fortunately feel invincible enough of the time to tackle things beyond our strength and our capabilities. Then there comes a day when whatever light you thought you saw ahead pales and you wonder where you were going in the first place.

Sarah McClendon Murphy has for some years, especially since her death in 1954, been a legendary figure in the South — a sort of black saint. I knew about her and admired her for the work she was doing but the day she stopped being a legend and became a tired, scared, terribly human and altogether heroic woman to me was the day a Negro schoolteacher told me about "Mama Sarah's dollar."

To go back, Sarah McClendon was the daughter of former slaves, Gabriel and Huldah McClendon, who were teen-agers living on a farm in Polk county Georgia "when freedom come in '65." She was the tenth of their eleven children and by the time her younger brother James was born in 1894 she was already acting like a little mother although she was only two. Their mother died when Sarah was four and James was two and although their father later brought them a stepmother, Ellen James, a good, loving, kind woman, Sarah early assumed a share of the responsibility of helping out with the children.

She was no more than twelve years old when she started "ordering off for flavorings" and selling them to make money to buy things for her sisters and brothers, James, seventy-five in 1969, remembers.

The only school available to them was a little country school, probably not particularly good in those days of untrained teachers and haphazard terms for Negroes whose labor was needed in the fields. But Sarah early showed an aptitude for learning that surprised even her family.

"She was way up in her books," James puts it.

When she finished what the country school had to offer, at the age of thirteen she began to work her way through an industrial school for Negroes in Rome, the Georgia city closest to the farm.

"She was always smart, always ahead," James said.

When she completed the courses offered in the industrial school she got a job teaching for the sum of eighteen dollars a month. It was a summer job and she had a hundred pupils during "lay-by time," that period in the summertime when the crops are in and tended and there's nothing more to be done until the harvest.

Out of her eighteen dollars pay Sarah started saving to go to Atlanta to the big Negro university complex. James, seventeen, was sympathetic to her dream. He left the farm and got a job on the railroad to help her.

Things were easier for Sarah in Atlanta. There were no farm chores to do, the academic life was pleasant and she enjoyed the sociability of the campus, the association of other young Negroes like herself who were thirsty for learning and the stimulation of the professors, both white and Negro. It occurred to her that she could stay in Atlanta and have a little rest and comfort for the first time in her life. Nobody knows for sure the conflicts that beset the young Negro girl at that time or the guilt that she felt over seeking for herself. But many people have heard of the dream she had one night during her student days at Spelman. Sarah was later to regard it as a vision.

She dreamed, she said, that she was walking "alongside a great canal."

"It was deep and swift and on the other side was a fence. There was a woman in the canal digging the ground out from under me about as fast as I could walk. I was fenced in all around. Then I came to a gate. I heard a voice say, 'Go through the gate, Sarah, and help your people.'"

Sarah had no trouble knowing who her people were — Negroes, country Negroes.

She herself had been luckier than most of her neighbors. Her father, "well-learned," as James says, for his time, was a good farmer and he supplemented his income by what they called "public work," which is to say any work off the farm. Her stepmother, half white

11

and never a slave, had been trained in all the domestic skills and had some education. So they had a great respect for learning and they wanted it for their children.

But even industrious, ambitious people like the McClendons had to scratch for a living. When James went to town to peddle the milk, butter and eggs that Ellen produced he felt lucky if he could bring home five cents a gallon for the milk, ten cents for a pound of butter and ten cents for a dozen eggs. A man lucky enough to get public work was content if he made sixty-five cents a day.

Public schools for Negroes were few and far between and Sarah began by teaching what they called an "independent" school in a church house.

"Parents was supposed to pay fifty cents a month," James remembers, "and they did if they had it. Sarah taught the children anyhow. She taught and she sang. Sarah was a mighty good singer — a note singer. Went to every singing convention she could and loved the gospel hymns. I can hear her now singing, 'I'm Thinking Today of Friends I Used to Know.'"

While she was teaching in an iron ore mining settlement near Rockmart Sarah met and soon married Marion Murphy. Marion, called "Shug" by family and friends, was the son of one of the men who contracted with the mining company to haul out ore by mule team from the mine to the little narrow gauge railroad trains which hauled it to the mills. From the engineer on one of these little trains Marion and Sarah bought their home — an old frame five-room house with an acre of land, costing them a total of two hundred dollars.

Later they were able to acquire more land — two or three eighty-acre parcels, one across the road from their house, another "out in the rural," as James says.

It was cheap, James remembers, because it was "either hilly land or land that wasn't so hilly but wasn't prosperous land, wasn't took care of."

They had been married five years when their first child was born, a little girl who Sarah named Divinia. She was the delight of her parents and their vast family connection.

"Papa had eleven children but mighty few grandchildren," James said, "and it looked like that made Sarah's baby extra precious. She was a good child, mannerly and friendly and, like Sarah, fast to learn."

Sarah was determined that Divinia would have a good education, but about the time the little girl was born their income was drastically cut. Marion was working in a quarry, breaking rock, and a sharp fragment flew up and hit him in the eye. He was incapacitated for weeks and eventually lost the eye — this to a man who had never heard of workmen's compensation or accident insurance.

Marion could farm. He and Sarah both loved the land. But cash money for a long time had to come through Sarah's efforts and it would take cash money to get Divinia an education. So Sarah went back to school. Every summer for years saw her at Spelman working to improve her teacher's certificate and eventually get a degree. She left Divinia with her stepmother or an older sister at these times.

By the time Divinia was nine years old, Marion was working in a cement plant for twenty-three cents an

13

hour and Sarah's pay from the county was up to about seventy-five dollars a month. She was teaching in a one-room school across the road from their house and taking Divinia with her.

There's no record of what happened to Divinia. James remembers that one day the little girl complained that one of her fingers hurt. But there was no sign of injury and no swelling. The pain simply became worse and two days later the child was dead.

"All we know," James said, "is what the undertaker said. He said it was blood poisoning."

Sarah was inconsolable. Her family and her husband talked to her of God's will and meeting Divinia one day in heaven but Sarah could only cry and walk the floor in an agony of grief. The loss of Divinia seemed to her to be harsh punishment with no reason behind it. She could not reconcile herself to it.

Like many a woman before her, Sarah may have been bitter the night she got word that a neighbor, brought to bed for her sixth childbearing, was bad off. The woman's husband had left home. There was no food for the sick woman, the new baby or the other five children. It must have seemed senseless and foreign to any divine plan in which she had believed for six children to be alive in want and neglect while her beloved Divinia, her only child, had died in spite of the loving care of two parents.

The mother of the six little Johnsons died that night, despite all Sarah could do. At daybreak, spent and weary, she left the body of the dead woman to the attention of other neighbors, bundled up the new baby, gathered the five older children to her and took them down the road to her house.

That was when Sarah became "Mama Sarah."

Three years later six more children arrived, shepherded along by their frightened mother. Her husband had died and she didn't know where to turn or what to do.

"You come right in here," said Mama Sarah. "We'll make room."

The little five-room house was getting crowded but not so crowded as it was to get.

"Folks commenced piling chillun on her," James said. "Sending and bringing."

James decided to have a talk with his sister about it. Marion was working hard on the farm and in the cement plant and Sarah was pushing herself harder than ever and there was still barely enough food to go around. There was a limit to what they could do and Sarah owed it to herself and her husband to draw the line somewhere.

That's when Sarah explained about her "vision," the dream she'd had at Spelman.

She had thought it meant for her to teach her people. But it must have meant a great deal more. "Go through the gate and help your people" must have meant to feed and clothe and shelter little children and to teach them to help themselves. It could have been intended that she would do for Negroes what Martha Berry had done for poor white children of the southern mountains.

James didn't remonstrate with her any more. But he knew that she and Marion had rough times.

One of her children, grown-up Susie Dorsey, told

15

me about it.

"I remember one time we didn't have nothing left in the house excepting some flour and a little meal. Didn't even have lard to make bread but we made it anyhow with just water. Then we browned some meal on the fire and stirred some water into it and made a gravy to eat on the flour bread."

Help always came and Sarah wouldn't let the children worry. Hunger was a temporary inconvenience, she told them, gathering them to her and teaching them songs and Bible verses. If they fed their minds on the beauty of Psalms and their spirits on belief in God's wonders they wouldn't notice so much that their stomachs were growling.

But more children continued to come — forty-two of them in the house at one time! — and her pay check and Marion's wouldn't begin to go around. One fall day between paydays Sarah's towering spirit toppled. Doubt took hold of her. The house teemed with children, all hungry, all needing things. Hers and Marion's last pay checks had vanished faster than the frost at sunup. The land, even with the help of the children, didn't produce enough to feed them all year. Hand-me-down clothes, collected from white friends in Rockmart and made over to fit the children, wore out and shoes for cold winter days were always a problem. When there was illness and a doctor had to be called — and Sarah, remembering Divinia, didn't hesitate to send for the doctor — the bill haunted her for months until she could pay it.

Maybe she was no Martha Berry after all. Maybe she was just a poor Negro schoolteacher who had delusions about her place in life.

Sarah decided to put it up to the Lord she had believed in and trusted all her life. She got down on her knees and prayed.

"If I'm intended to go on, God," she said, "send me a sign. A dollar, God, send just one dollar."

Praying usually comforted her, but in a way she had delivered an ultimatum to the Lord and it made her restless and uneasy. She did an unaccustomed thing. She took a walk by herself, with no covey or cluster of little children milling around her or clinging to her hands.

But when she came back one of them ran to meet her. He was a little boy and he was waving a crumpled dirty one-dollar bill.

"Look what I found by the railroad track, Mama Sarah!" he cried.

It was the sign Sarah needed to keep going.

Laughing and crying, she hugged the little boy to her and went into the house to put on the last potatoes for their supper.

The old house was stretched by the addition of wooden work trailers begged from the county and converted to dormitories for the boys. Sarah and Shug had started out to keep a bedroom for themselves but it speedily caught the overflow of cots and pallets and they soon felt lucky if they could sleep the night through without two or three wet or chilly youngsters crawling into bed with them.

There was room, if they had to have it, Sarah said — and they kept having to have it.

"I remember one cold December night we were up

late canning some fruit somebody had brought us," Susie Dorsey said. "We heard footsteps running across the front porch and one of the bigger girls went to the door. At first she thought nobody was there but then she saw a box with a baby in it."

Mama Sarah was delighted. She complied with the legalities by sending somebody to notify the Rockmart police, but the baby was hers to keep. She knew it and the police, having no other place to send a Negro baby in any case, concurred.

"We named the baby 'Frosty Night,'" Mrs. Dorsey said. "She kept that name until she was grown. Now she calls herself Margaret instead of Frosty. I know. She's my sister-in-law. We married brothers."

Sarah had many friends, white and black, but none better than Mr. and Mrs. Rufus L. Campbell of Rockmart. They watched her work with interest and admiration and helped her when they could. Ruby Campbell came from a newspapering family and she kept her hand in by writing occasional pieces for the local weekly and serving as correspondent for the Atlanta dailies. Her stories about Mama Sarah's little cottage industry — a burgeoning orphanage — brought various kinds of help, clothes, a sack of flour, an occasional check. The city of Rockmart gave her twenty-five dollars a month. Polk County commissioners voted to match it. One Negro church pledged two dollars a month out of its pitiful treasury, another one dollar. An occasional expatriate Rockmart citizen would latch on to one of Mrs. Campbell's stories about Mama Sarah and send a contribution, some of them sustaining contributions which continue to this day.

Then in 1946, what seemed to her to be astonishing overwhelming good fortune came to Mama Sarah.

Mrs. Campbell nominated her for the radio Good Neighbor Award offered on Tom Breneman's "Breakfast in Hollywood" radio show. Sarah won the award and the delighted Campbells went to Chicago with her to see her feted on a nationwide hookup, to attend the première of the movie *Breakfast in Hollywood* and to receive a $1,000 check.

Sarah loved the trip, the sightseeing, the parties. She choked up over national recognition of her work. But the check, the beautiful $1,000 check, was like the dollar of her prayer — a sign, a divine direction. It meant that her children would have a real home, bigger, safer, more comfortable. She dreamed of indoor plumbing and steam heat and she gave the place a name — a real name. It would be named for her little lost daughter, Divinia.

Back in Rockmart, Sarah put the $1,000 check in a bank account which was to be the nucleus of a building fund. She would make a public appeal, sell some land, enlist the help of the Campbells and all her other friends.

The national publicity received on the radio show would help. And it did help. Contributions to the building fund were beginning to come in when tragedy struck.

Sarah went into town one day to see a doctor about a pain that had been bothering her in her chest. While she was absent the old house caught fire from the wood stove in the kitchen and burned down. Marion and the older children got all of the children out except one —

a little baby in a crib.

The death of the baby plunged Sarah into a new abyss of grief but it dramatized for outsiders the scope of the job she was trying to do. The trickle of help broadened to a stream. Friends and neighbors arrived and helped Sarah and Shug set up beds and a stove in the schoolhouse across the road. Contributions came winging in — food, clothes, money. Within a short time the building fund grew to $45,000. Lumber and bricks and workmen started arriving.

Shug died before the new building was finished. A few months later when it was ready for partial occupancy, Sarah walked over the yard, directing the children in a raking, tidying operation. She leaned over to pick up some scraps of lumber and the old pain in her chest struck again. She died before they could summon help.

The home was finished — named for Sarah and Divinia. A chuch group came forward to run it. It is clean and spacious with an ample playground, and Spelman and Morris Brown College students come in the summer to coach the children on subjects they find difficult in the now integrated Rockmart public schools. They have a little library and toys and games and nourishing meals.

The name Sarah Murphy is a name and little more to the children. But to Susie Dorsey, helping out in the dining room, it means safety and love and confidence in the future.

Sarah's little talks come back to her often — the emphasis on cleanliness, the responsibility to share what you have, not with just your own people but with the hungry white people down the road, the duty to clean up around your own door and beyond.

"She never stopped when she got our yard raked and clean. She went on until we had cleaned the schoolyard and the churchyard and all up and down the road, her leading and working as hard as the rest of us. . . . We had to bathe every night, no matter what. We just had a tin washtub and we had to draw water out of the well and warm it on the stove but we had to be clean. She told us, 'If your skin be black and clean you can be proud. But black and dirty, that won't do.'"

A portrait of Sarah hangs in the lobby of the new home. It was done by an Atlanta artist named Ouida Canaday, and I think Bishop Oxnam would feel that it outstrips Whistler's portrait of his mother four to one in one way. It shows three children crowded close to Mama Sarah and if you search the shadows behind the fine black head of the Negro woman in a certain light and from a certain distance you can see the face of another child. The shadowy, elusive little face is that of Divinia, the only child she ever gave birth to but the one who prepared her to give life to more than two hundred others.

Chapter 3

ON A WINDY MARCH day in 1940 motorists on the beach drive in the beautiful old Mississippi town of Biloxi saw a strange procession of small boats moving across the choppy waters of the inner harbor.

The little shrimp boat, the *Sea Queen*, led the way, her deck scrubbed, her paint gleaming and her hatch piled high with a great bank of flowers.

One at a time the others came — fishing boats and seagoing freight boats and, wallowing in their wake, skiffs and sailboats and little launches. They moved slowly, each one freighted with flowers which contrasted brilliantly with the somber garb of the people who ran the boats or rode on them.

At the foot of Oak Street the *Sea Queen* docked. The other boats tied up close by and their passengers climbed out and stood with heads bared and faces taut with grief as the boatmen moved forward and lifted the *Sea Queen's* cargo from its mooring of flowers.

Grandma Aken, the Gulf coast's most famous

islander, was on her way to a mainland resting place, the old Biloxi cemetery.

The hundreds of people who lined the docks and crowded into the historic Episcopal Church of the Redeemer for the funeral included friends and neighbors among the Biloxi townspeople and, of course, a sprinkling of the curious who had heard of but never seen the colorful old woman.

But a surprising number of them were Grandma Aken's own — her children, her grandchildren, her great- and great-great-grandchildren. For in the century she lived (actually one hundred years, six months, three days, her descendants say), Harriet Watters Baker Aken reared seventeen children of her own and twenty-five that she had adopted. Her own descendants numbered thirty-eight grandchildren, forty-one great-grandchildren and twelve great-great-grandchildren and nobody tried to count the children and grandchildren of that vast company of little strangers that Grandma "took to raise."

They came from all parts of the United States to pay homage to the fantastic, iron-willed, old saltwater matriarch.

Most of those in the funeral procession from Deer Island were Grandma's "boys" — island-reared fishermen and boatmen, their faces reddened by winter winds and nearly tropical summer suns, their hands roughened by icy lines, the leads on cast nets and oyster tongs.

They came out of love, loyalty and a fierce kind of gratitude.

But the old lady they were to bury was no lavender-scented, lace-fichued saint. There are no monuments to her now and there were no schools or hospitals or parks being named for her then. Her good works, far from being an inspiration to her fellow citizens, warmly applauded and financially supported by church and civic club, were sometimes subject to question.

Why did Harriet Aken always have *boys* with her? Her foster children numbered twenty-four boys and one girl. Why?

The answer was easy for her detractors: Work, of course. She gave a home and a living to boys so they could tend the cattle and butcher the meat, fish, and hunt and till the soil for her. Oh, sure, Grandma Aken was good to them, said the cynical. She had a free labor force. Why, that old lady was as tough as a marlin spike and as handy with shotgun and rifle as a man!

And like a lot of criticism it had truth in it — truth taken out of context and distorted and misunderstood.

Grandma Aken *did* take boys instead of girls to live with her on Deer Island and she *did* give them work, plenty of work, to do. She *was* as tough as a marlin spike and, as one of her grandchildren put it, not afraid of "anything or anybody, natural or supernatural."

She had dealt with Union soilders, Confederate deserters, snakes and hurricanes in her time and when her boys misbehaved she "laid the dogwood" to them without worrying a moment about warping their little personalities. When poachers moved in on her oyster beds she grabbed her rifle and ran them off, single-minded and comfortable with the knowledge that she might have to kill one or two to teach them a lesson.

Beyond these obvious and well-known truths, there was another known only to her own, her children and the forlorn little troop that came out of New Orleans orphanages, "asylums" and broken homes. There was in Harriet Aken a deep belief in children, in what they could do and what they could be. And there was boundless giving, of time and attention, of gaiety and good times, of such material things as she possessed.

Her detractors may have pointed out that it was ambitious charity since she wasn't a rich woman — not by the standards of the New Orleans millionaires whose white houses lined the beach drive. She certainly wasn't leisured, that doughty woman in the black skirt and the white "josie" blouse, who not only did all her own cooking, dishing up food for as many as forty people on Sunday, but raised, caught or killed most of it.

But she was richer than most of the rich and had time aplenty for what she considered important.

Harriet Watters married when she was twelve years old. She was the daughter of English settlers on Horn Island, Deer Island's neighbor to the southeast, and it was there that she met and married Peter Baker, the son of a lighthouse keeper. The young Bakers joined the older Watterses in the family cattle-raising enterprise on Horn Island, and later Harriet was to tell her children and grandchildren of their struggles to save their cows from the foraging Confederate soldiers first and then from the foraging Union forces when the Civil War started. The war was young when Harriet took her children and left Peter Baker.

Polite accounts of her life always say she "lost" him. Her granddaughter, Mrs. Ada Andrews, finds that an amusing delicacy since Grandma herself, unlike modern mothers, never tried to put a pretty face on her relationships. They separated and were divorced, says Mrs. Andrews, and this in a time when divorce was practically unheard of, particularly in the strongly Roman Catholic coastal towns.

Seafood and farm products were plentiful at their island home and the young mother had no difficulty feeding her family, especially since she didn't feel compelled to obey Confederate enjoiners against trafficking with the enemy. She had butter and eggs and fresh vegetables; the Yankees, who manned the gunboats anchored off neighboring Ship Island, had flour and sugar and coffee. Harriet took her provender and her children and under cover of darkness sailed out at night and effected a swap.

"She didn't care much for the Confederates anyhow," said Mrs. Andrews. (A bold statement in the town where Jefferson Davis lived out his final years, where his home, Beauvoir, is still a shrine, and where his pew is marked with a brass plate in Mrs. Andrews' own church.) "They confiscated her cows and sometimes deserters would hide out on one of the islands and she'd take her gun and sit up all night to protect her supplies and stock from them. I think she got along better with the Yankees."

Actually most of the other people along that stretch of southern coastline had a live-and-let-live arrangement with their northern enemy. The peace was shattered only once and that was when a small Federal patrol boat, traveling under a flag of truce, landed on the mainland at Biloxi to return a little girl it had rescued from a boat that had drifted out from shore. On the way back to Ship Island the patrol boat ran aground on Deer Island and some Southerners, apparently not understanding it had a mercy mission, opened fire on it with small arms.

When the tide rose and the patrol boat floated free the incident was duly reported to the Union garrison on Ship Island, where the commanding general saw it as the worst kind of violation of a truce. He ordered the immediate capture of Biloxi and three gunboats carrying a combined naval and army force of five hundred landed the next morning. Happily, the mayor met them with a handsome apology. Northern pride was placated and the Yankees returned to Ship Island without firing a shot.

About that time Harriet Baker was also aground on Deer Island, the beautiful five-mile stretch of white beaches, woods and Indian mounds that lies half a mile south of the Biloxi mainland.

She had married Joseph Aken, whose father, Albertus King Aken, bought 159 acres of the island from government bounty land in 1850, and whose mother, Jane, brought to the family estate 199 more island acres she acquired from the state of Mississippi for twenty-five cents each. They had a big turpentine operation on the island and Harriet and Joseph moved there to help them run it.

The house, made of cypress and yellow pine, is a rambling one-story building with a wide front verandah facing Biloxi across the bay and a detached kitchen facing the Mississippi Sound in the rear. Great mossy live oak trees, their dark branches twisted by a century of hurricane winds, sheltered the house and continue to shelter it today, although it is now boarded up and overgrown with a tangle of weeds and vines.

The island soil away from the beaches and the shell mounds, on which the house was built, was rich, and Harriet Aken was a natural gardener. She always said the benign winds from the gulf gentled winter temperatures so it was possible to grow fine oranges and figs and plums for the beautiful English plum puddings she made in the wintertime and an almost year-round succession of vegetables, corn, beans, okra for her seafood gumbos and seasonings for her celebrated court bouillon. ("Coo-biyon," Grandma's children call this baked fish dish.) She raised chicken and pork and beef for her own table and supplemented them with game which she hunted and killed as competently as any man.

With the boom of Biloxi as both a winter and summer resort about the turn of the century, the Akens found a ready market for their surplus at the Biloxi Yacht Club and the swank Montross Hotel. And Harriet herself was frequently seen rowing across the bay to deliver oysters, geese, ducks or homegrown vegetables.

Both sets of children, the young Bakers and the young Akens, grew up. Grandchildren were coming along and the old house was always filled with them and their friends, particularly in the summertime. Even so, when Harriet went with one of her daughters to visit a New Orleans orphanage one day she came home with a child — the first and only little girl she "took to raise."

Rhoda Louise Williams was eight years old. Her father had died at sea. Her mother died shortly afterward and no relatives came forward to claim her.

Something about the little girl went straight to Harriet's heart. The child, now seventy-three and one of only a handful of Grandma's children surviving, remembers it as a mystical moment when the old lady saw her, loved her and determined to have her for her own.

It was her special gift, this quality of making each child feel singled out, chosen.

"She chose me from one hundred and fifty orphans," an old man remembers. "I was ten years old. I never knew my father. My mother had to put me in a juvenile home. Grandma Aken saw me and I don't know why, with all those other boys there, but that was it: I was the one."

Over and over again Biloxi people saw the sturdy old woman get off the train holding a child's hand, or meeting a train to welcome a child. People heard of her and sent her children. Even Biloxi children who had good homes and devoted parents sometimes showed up on the island and stayed for weeks, touching home base on Saturdays when all the bigger children rowed to the mainland with their twenty-five cents' allowance to "go to the show."

Work, hard work and long hours of it, was the portion of every child on the island, but much of it was what would pass for recreation a generation later.

Knowing how to swim was a necessity for islanders. Grandma, expert herself long before it became stylish for "nice" women to know how to swim, remembered the loss of a son from a fishing boat with a deep sense of grief and she taught all her young wards well. Rowing a boat to the mainland for kerosene and flour was fun and Grandma didn't mind if children dawdled a little but not to the detriment of her groceries.

"She sent me for meat one time when we ran out in the summertime and I got to playing chinies with some boys and nearly let it spoil in the heat. When I got back she laid the dogwood to me!"

It was just punishment, the boy recognized then, and was typical of Harriet.

"She only whipped you when you needed it," her children and grandchildren report. And sometimes when it was a borderline case Grandpa Aken would intervene with an "Aw, Hannah . . . !" (his name for her). Grandma would good-naturedly abandon the switch with a warning and take off on some project of her own.

She hated housework, except for cooking.

"She was much more at home with a cast net or a shotgun than she was in the house," her children will tell you. "But when it comes to cooking, ah, how she loved to feed people!"

Casual about religion herself, she was meticulous about sending her children across the bay to church and Sunday school and cheerfully paid tuition to a parochial school for those among her foster children who were Roman Catholics. She was confirmed in the Episcopal Church, but the bishop came to the island

31

for the service, instead of vice versa. Once a month the rector of the Church of the Redeemer would row over to visit and would hold a service if Grandma's household numbered enough people at the time to warrant it. If the Catholic children had to miss school because of illness the nuns from the convent frequently rowed over to see them.

"Grandma always made them stay for a wonderful supper. She didn't make many frosted cakes but she could walk up to that old woodstove and turn out a pound cake or an apple dumpling or a boiled pudding that you'd never forget. She cooked Spanish and French and some English, too, because, of course, her parents were English."

Until he died in 1913 Joseph was always amused at visitors who expected life on the island to be austere. He had a stock answer for strangers who asked, "What do you find to eat?"

"South wind and sand pudding," Joseph replied.

Grandma was seventy-three when Joseph died and thought to be an old woman by her children and grandchildren. Her widowed daughter, Mrs. Ella Thompson, moved in with her and grandchildren built houses close by for company. But Harriet was healthy and vigorous and such ills as she had she treated with poultices and teas brewed out of her own little collection of herbs and medicinal plants. Her weathered old face became marked with sores her children thought were skin cancer and they urged her to let them take her across the bay to a doctor or into New Orleans to a celebrated cancer clinic.

She said she didn't have time, she'd take care of her

complexion herself. Whatever she used, it worked and she had energy left over for taking more orphans to rear.

Quarter of a century before her death she gave up going to the mainland. She had outlived all her old friends.

"I walked all over town," she complained to her daughter Ella, "and I only saw three people I knew."

There was so much to do on the island. The weather was both her friend and her adversary and she had to teach all her children how to get ready for those autumnal hurricanes, at least one of which was usually expected to cover the thin sliver of sand and woodland completely. Hurricane Camille finally did destroy the house in 1969 but this was, of course, after Grandma Aken died. Before a storm actually struck the coast Grandma would be ready for it and pacing the beach to watch it arrive.

"She could tell by the pelicans," one of her foster children said. "When they came into the bay she started preparing."

She would lay in a supply of candles and cook food that would keep and taste good cold because a fire in the stove was risky in winds of hurricane force. She would drive the cattle to the high ground and have the boys secure the boats and then she would relax and enjoy the electric excitement of brutal winds and churning water.

She had little formal learning to pass on to her charges. She didn't philosophize or preach. She had an even cheerful disposition and she took it for granted that all the members of her household would have the same. She worked and believed that the ability to work prepared them for life away from the island. "Learn to do at least one thing well," she said, "and when you can better yourself I want you to go."

An old man, now retired, sat alone watching television cartoons in a little house on a back street in Biloxi. He had known want and uncertainty and the quirks and caprices of those who ran juvenile homes before Grandma "picked me." He tried to put his feeling about her into words.

He remembered much and was grateful for much and then he achieved real eloquence.

"She never, never, *never* let you go to bed hungry!" he said in a tone which made that a matchless achievement for any woman.

Chapter 4

MOTHERS, AS HAS oft been demonstrated, will do anything for their children. I used to write confession stories for mine. Oh, not for them to read, of course, but to buy something the budget wouldn't dream of covering or to pay for something the budget should have covered but had shiftily side-stepped.

Sometimes the cut-off man from the waterworks or the power or gas company would be hovering at the threshold even as I put the finishing touches to a stirring opus entitled "I Stole My Sister's Husband," "I was a Junkie" or "I Loved the Man Who Killed My Husband."

They were terrible stories but the pay seemed munificent at the time and I didn't give them up until I met a young woman I'll call Cora Purefoy and wrote a little gem entitled "I Sold My Baby for $300."

At the time I covered the courthouse for our newspaper and, as every old courthouse reporter knows, that beat pulses and throbs with human drama. People don't go to the courthouse, except sometimes to pay their taxes or to nag the zoning board, unless they are in big trouble.

The day I met a lanky old mountain man and his shy, doelike little sixteen-year-old daughter Cora on the courthouse steps, the aura of trouble was unmistakable. They looked about them in confusion and distress and I asked them if I could help them.

The father looked at me appraisingly, looked at his daughter and looked back at me.

"Which judge gits young'uns back?" he asked.

"I want my baby!" whimpered the girl.

"We come to git Cora's young'un," affirmed the father. "We want to do it right. We got us a lawyer."

It occurred to me that the alternative to a lawyer might be a shotgun, and hastily, before the old man's resolve to "do it right" should evaporate, I led them to juvenile court. There the lawyer waited and there the Purefoys eventually emerged triumphant with a few-months-old infant Cora had mistakenly sold to its father and his wife for three hundred dollars before the child was born.

The confession magazine for which I occasionally contrived a pretty trifle had heard of the story. (I can imagine how. It was only on the front page of our newspaper and the "A" wire of a couple of news services.) In a day or two I had a telegram asking me if I would see Cora and "ghost" a first-person account of her experience for them — the title, of course, to be "I Sold My Baby for $300."

It didn't seem likely to me that the Purefoys would want further publicity but I called the lawyer and he and his wife agreed to drive up to the mountains with me to see.

The old house, sparsely furnished but immaculate from sweeping and scrubbing, sat in the middle of a field in a beautiful valley far back in the hills. Flowers bloomed in the front yard, chickens scratched and clucked in the back, and there were children of all ages all over the place.

I knew the bare bones of the story. Cora had been hired by Fred and Annie, some former neighbors who had moved from the hill country to an Atlanta cotton mill village, to live in their house and "do" for the wife, who was poorly. After she got to town the wife's condition worsened and while she was in the hosptial the husband seduced Cora.

When the wife came home, Cora, noticeably pregnant, departed and, not wishing to shame her parents, found refuge with friends in a little mountain town far from home. Her seducer and his wife had no children themselves and they talked over the matter of Cora's approaching accouchement. If they paid the lying-in expenses maybe Cora would give them the baby?

From where Cora sat at that moment it looked like a good deal. Unborn, the baby was obviously a costly piece of merchandise she couldn't afford. She took the three hundred dollars and gave the couple a lien, duly signed. The day after the birth of the baby the lien holders arrived with the local sheriff and a possessory warrant to claim their property, somewhat like a loan shark repossessing an old washing machine on which the payments were delinquent.

By that time Cora had looked on her little son and

changed her mind.

She appealed to her parents, who appealed to an Atlanta judge and there was the little fellow fanning the air with his hands and gurgling happily on a pallet on the floor of his grandparents' house.

To turn out a confession story about it I needed Cora's cooperation and her parents' consent, since she was a minor. I explained this to Cora and her mother, a little woman who, like the house, seemed to have been faded an indeterminate gray by time and the weather.

"You'll have to ask Popper," said the mother. "He's adoin' public work. He'll be home to supper t'reckly."

In due time I saw "Popper" swinging down the road from his job as a rock mason on a new motel. He had his dinner bucket in his hand, not a squirrel rifle, but I had a nervous feeling that he wasn't going to take kindly to having his daughter's shame exploited in a confession magazine.

He was cordial in a gruff, shy countryman's way and that made it all the harder for me to drag out the telegram and present the proposition to him.

"They'll pay me to write Cora's story," I explained hesitantly. "And they'll pay Cora for signing it — fifty dollars for a short story, seventy-five dollars for a long one."

He looked at the ground and swallowed hard. Then he looked off toward the line of blue hills which cupped the valley. He spat into some weeds and faced me with an expression of stern resolve.

"All I got to say," he said finally, "is make it a long 'un."

As all confession writers learn, the people who have

lush, lurid or, at any rate, salable experiences are usually inarticulate. I needed all kinds of details from Cora and she tried to be helpful but it was difficult to talk to her with her parents, her lawyer, her baby and half a dozen younger brothers and sisters sitting around the room listening.

We laboriously worked over the territory of her background, her childhood, everything leading up to her departure for the city with Fred and Annie. Then we got to the seduction and, knowing my market, I really did need some details.

"Now, Cora," I began, "tell me *how it was?*"

"What do you mean 'how it was?'" asked the girl.

"I mean," I tried again, "the night that he *came to you.*"

"She means when he overpowered you, Cora!" cried the mother impatiently.

I don't know if Cora couldn't remember or if, with her audience being what it was, she couldn't find the words. But I finally gave up and decided to rely on my own imagination.

A couple of weeks later the lawyer and I went back to the mountains with the finished story for the Purefoys' approval and signature on the release. Popper was at home that day and when I handed him the story he and his wife looked at one another helplessly and she finally said, "Would you read it to us?" Before I could get started, the room began filling up. All the family and, I suspect, some of the neighbors had gathered for "the readin' of Cora's story." They filled the chairs, the window sill, the floor and lined up beside Cora on the edge of the bed.

The reading went pretty well at first. I love the mountains and mountain people and I got in some description I privately thought was far too good for a confession magazine.

The Purefoys listened impassively.

Then I hit the seduction scene. I looked at the fifteen-year-old brother and the granite-faced old father and my throat grew scratchy and my palms grew wet. The squirrel rifle was hanging on the wall in full view but I didn't know anything to do but read doggedly on. I clutched the pages harder and plunged in: "I felt his hot breath upon my cheek, his hands pinioning me to the mattress. . . ."

Mrs. Purefoy flung her apron over her head and started crying. Cora fell down across the bed and muffled her sobs in a pillow.

Nobody else spoke.

I read on.

When it was over I waited apprehensively.

The mother pulled the apron off her face and said warmly, "I know in my soul that's as purty a story as I ever heerd!"

Cora pulled her face out of the pillow and smiled on me rosily and Popper stood up and said importantly, "We'll want a copy of that in the magyzine."

When Cora's story came out in the magazine and my copy came I read it fast and routinely got it out of the house. (Trash paid but I didn't want my children reading it.) But before I wrapped it in a brown paper and put it in the garbage can I reread it and Cora's decision about the baby was so simple and so right I felt a rush of deep admiration for her and deep regret over exposing her to the avid readers of the confession market. It would be the last such story I would write.

"I seen hit," she said of the baby, "and I loved hit right away. I knowed I'd spend the rest of my life trying to be good enough and raise hit right."

What mother could say more?

— sad stories. But after a day or two my conscience hurt me and I went looking for the Purcells and their little girl.

They had left the private infirmary where they had received the death-or-blindness diagnosis and gone to the city-county charity hospital, Grady, in the hope of finding better news. I found them in the children's ward there — Frank, the father, a quiet, country-reared man of forty, who had recently been laid off by a small-town textile mill, and his wife, Montell, thirty-three. They sat beside the bed of a frisky, beautiful little girl named Carolyn, who had bright brown eyes and hair to match curling around a piquant face and pulled into a pigtail in the back.

They told me the story.

Carolyn was their only child and although they had to work hard for everything they had, at Christmastime they took special pleasure in buying their little girl everything they dreamed she would like. Before Frank was laid off at the mill Montell had bought and put away Carolyn's Christmas toys and they both felt relieved and happy that the specter of unemployment wouldn't mar Christmas morning at their house. One of the presents Montell was happiest over and the one that cost the most was a new tricycle. Carolyn had seen tricycles and had talked of nothing else in all the weeks leading up to Christmas.

When Christmas morning dawned the child was out of bed before her father could get up and build a fire. She went straight for the Christmas tree and, stumbling a little (her mother thought from excitement), she found the doll. She looked around and at and over

46

Chapter 5

THE DECISIONS INVOLVED in being a mother are sometimes so frightening you wonder how any woman has the courage to make them. The most courageous woman I ever saw was a big-eyed country girl named Montell Purcell. She took the responsibility of a life-and-death or, as the newspaper called it at the time, death-or-blindness decision on herself.

It was New Year's Eve 1951 when I first heard of the Purcells. A friend whose husband was in the hospital called and told me that while she was waiting out her husband's operation she got to talking to a woman whose five-year-old daughter was in the hospital to have her eyes checked.

"That little girl, that *baby*, has cancer!" cried my friend. "The doctor just told the mother she will have to have her eyes removed or she will die!"

It was what used to be known as a human-interest story and I didn't have much heart for it. It was the holiday season and nobody wants to read — or to write the new tricycle — without seeing it.

"She didn't know it was there," her mother said chokily. "The tricycle she wanted so bad."

As the morning passed and Carolyn gradually discovered and played with her toys, Frank and Montell, looking at each other fearfully, began to realize that their little girl, the child with the bright, beautiful eyes, couldn't see.

They had little money and they knew almost nothing about getting around Atlanta, although they had grown up and lived all their adult lives less than fifty miles from the city limits. But they were undaunted in their determination to find the best medical help for Carolyn. I found out later the reason they acted so swiftly was that their first child, a little girl named Mary Marjorie, had died without medical attention of what the father called "a kind of mystery disease" ten years before Carolyn was born. The day after Christmas they took Carolyn to a country doctor who recommended a city specialist and arranged an appointment for them.

It was at the ear-eyes-nose-throat infirmary that they learned for the first time that Carolyn's trouble was not simple nearsightedness which could be corrected by glasses but something which could cost her life. The name the doctor gave it was glioma.

Hoping against hope that the doctor was mistaken, they had come to Grady, the hospital where most Atlanta doctors teach or serve on the staff as consultants. When I found them, Carolyn was being given a series of tests and was being examined by five or six of the city's other leading eye specialists.

47

They had been in the hospital for two or three days when the results of a clinic held by the entire staff on opthamalogy were made known. A group of reporters had gathered and we stood in the hall with Montell and her parents when an intern brought up the report, a written diagnosis, and read it to them. It said, in effect, that the child did indeed have glioma, that she would have to lose one eye immediately and the other one probably very soon.

There hadn't been much real hope in the Purcells and in Montell's family, the Dinsmores. They were resigned to the operation. Frank, looking stricken, saw no other course.

Surprisingly, when we all turned to Montell, her answer was a low-voiced, "No."

A delay, the young intern explained patiently, might be dangerous.

"No," said Montell again. "We'll wait."

That night she and Frank took Carolyn and, against the doctors' advice, left the hospital. They went to the home of some relatives who ran a truck stop on a four-lane highway twenty miles north of Atlanta. I saw them almost daily and I felt close enough to Montell to ask her how she dared to wait. She was a woman of little education and, of course, no medical skill. How dare she pit her knowledge against the best medical opinion available in the hospitals and medical schools of our town?

It was then she told me about Mary Marjorie.

She and Frank were very young and very poor when Mary Marjorie was born. They lived on a farm in one of the mountain counties, miles from the nearest doctor and with no car. One day the little girl got sick. All day long Montell nursed her, using such home remedies as she knew about, and steadily the child grew worse.

Frank started walking for help and along about dusk he came back home with a borrowed truck. They wrapped Mary Marjorie up and started to the nearest doctor. The child died on the way.

"I know the Lord don't always answer you the way you want Him to," Montell said, "but I believe He answers you. All day long I prayed that He would make my baby well. He didn't answer my prayer that way but I felt He had a purpose and when the answer come I could take it. I'm praying now and I got to wait."

While Montell waited, people all over the world seemed stirred by the story. Soldiers in Korea wrote her, expressing sympathy and encouragement. Convicts in prisons offered their eyes. Some people urged the operation, some warned her against it. The great Helen Keller wrote and told her not to be afraid, blindness was not so bad, a child could give up her eyes and still have a good life. Advice poured in from every corner of the world. Faith healers came and marched and prayed and sang in the yard. Sightseers came just to look at the child and her parents.

And through it all, Montell, a real gentlewoman, held up her head and smiled and thanked people. And waited.

After about a week, Fred Cannon, head of the local Shrine Horse Patrol, called me and said he had been reading the stories about Carolyn and he and his fellow Shriners were deeply concerned. They had no doubt

49

that the child should have the operation but they understood the mother's reluctance and they felt that another diagnosis from a high-placed source would help her decide. Would I ask her if she would take the child to the Mayo Clinic if I would go with her and the Shriners would pay the expense of the trip?

Both Frank and Montell were overwhelmed by the offer. I could see in Montell's white face the hungry hope that this was "the answer."

Gifts for the child came pouring in. "Papa Sunshine," a Jewish immigrant who ran a department store in a poor section of town, outfitted her with new clothes and a warm coat with a hat that had earmuffs for the cold Minnesota weather. There were toys and gifts of money and a big crowd gathered at the airport to see us off on a gray January day.

Carolyn was bouncy and bright-eyed, and Montell, although tired and pale, smiled a lot. And I privately worried that the child might die on the trip.

Wherever the plane stopped — and they were making more stops in 1951 — people came out to greet Carolyn and to give her presents or to shout advice to her mother. Not once did Montell plead weariness or fail to smile and express her gratitude. It was night when we landed in Rochester and although the Shriners, wearing their cheery red fezzes, came out to meet us and to take us to the hotel adjoining the big clinic, it did seem a foreign land to all three of us. All that snow and ice, that unbroken, unrelenting whiteness.

The next day we learned that such examinations as Carolyn's take time and it might be several days before they could begin hers. In the meantime, we were to wait. Having a job and children of my own to worry about, I started making arrangements to turn Montell and Carolyn over to the hospital social service people when I saw Montell's courage falter a little. She had been so brave and so strong but she couldn't bear to be left alone now.

The social workers saw it too, and suddenly, miraculously, somebody stamped Carolyn's case "Emergency" and the next morning at daybreak she began her trip through that vast clinic.

All day long the child and her mother went from test to test, from examination to examination. I was waiting for them at dusk in a little room on the ground floor of the clinic. The lights had not been turned on but there was a strange, silvery twilight reflected from the snow outside. I stood at the window looking at the whiteness and the roof line of a little church strung with icicles.

Montell came in quietly. Carolyn, exhausted from the day's ordeal, was asleep in her mother's arms. Montell held in her hand a piece of paper on which somebody had written the verdict.

"Would you read it for me?" she asked.

I took the paper to the window and read. The child did not have cancer, she did not need to lose her eyes. The difficulty she had was caused by a nutritional deficiency. She could go home and be treated in Atlanta.

I looked up and Montell was looking out the window at the little church, with tears streaming down her cheeks.

"Thank you, Lord," she whispered. "I knowed You'd

51

tell me."

Some people believe in miracles. I'm not sure that I do but Montell Purcell does. She said later, "You know all them doctors couldn't have been wrong. The Lord worked a miracle, He did."

If miracles exist, a stubborn, believing mother waited one out for Carolyn. Today Carolyn is a beautiful young married woman with a three-year-old daughter, Stephanie. Frank died in September 1968 and Montell now spends a lot of time with Carolyn and her family and smiles her warm, serene smile when friends remark that Carolyn's eyes are her prettiest feature.

"Did you know," she murmurs with a touch of awe, "she has twenty-twenty vision?"

Chapter 6

ONE OF THE BEST mothers I ever knew was a team of men — a young white man I'll call Joe and an old black man I'll call Horace. Their "mothering" of five boys — Joe's brothers — whose parents were killed in an automobile accident, impressed me and everybody who knew about it.

It was after the double funeral that the family gathered at the boys' home and gravitated gradually to the back porch, where old Mister Alex, the family lawyer for many years, had decided to hold conference.

"What are we going to do with these children?" he asked the assembly of aunts, uncles and cousins.

Joe, the eldest of the six sons, was on his knees in the backyard gathering mint for the juleps, which his father had always served when the family assembled. He reared back on his heels and looked up at the group.

An aunt offered to take one of the younger boys

whose age matched that of her son. She theorized that they would attend school together and become chums, although up until that time they had detested one another. A family friend from Mississippi delta country said he could use a couple of the older boys on his plantation, since they probably weren't going to be able to go to college anyhow. An elderly woman cousin, a widow who lived in one of the bigger and handsomer houses in town, said she adored the boys and would do everything in her power to help them, short of having them move in with her.

"If they were only little girls," she said, sighing. "I am too old for all that boy-boisterousness."

Joe, listening, smiled. There was some boy-boisterousness involved, of course. But Stevie, the youngest of the brothers, had just turned seven, a gentle dreamy little fellow who had discovered books and spent hours reading. And Ed, ten, who had had rheumatic fever . . . Joe's heart turned over every time he thought of him, thin and pale and quiet, his health a constant concern to their parents. Of course, the others — Chuck, twelve, Ben, fourteen, Paul, sixteen — were in rugged health and what you might call boisterous.

Joe stood up and faced the group on the porch.

"Mister Alex," he said, "thank you, sir. And thank you all for your offers. But the boys and I will stay right here, together. This is our home so . . . it's where we'll stay."

"Ah, Joe," protested one of the women. "You know you can't raise these boys. Why, you're nothing but a boy yourself, still in school."

"What are you, son, nineteen?" asked the lawyer.

"Yes, sir," said Joe. "Almost."

"And you've got three more years at the university?"
Joe nodded.

"Well, you can't take care of this family, that's all
there is to it," put in a cousin.

"I've got to do it," Joe said stubbornly. "We're not
going to be separated. I'll think of something."

The mint juleps were served and Horace, a black
servant who had been with the boys' parents since their
marriage, set out the funeral foods neighbors had
brought in. The six brothers, subdued and neat in
their dark Sunday suits, moved among their relatives
receiving condolences self-consciously. One by one the
departing relatives spoke to Joe, repeating the ancient
litany so familiar to the troubled and bereaved: "If
there is anything I can do . . ."

One person made the offer precise and specific:
Horace. As they cleaned up the kitchen together, Joe
tried haltingly to tell Horace that there wasn't going to
be much money. His father, still young, had been just
getting started in a new business. The car, which
Horace had kept in order and driven when their
mother needed to go out, had been destroyed in the
accident. The yard and housecleaning chores, for-
merly done by Horace, would have to be done by the
boys themselves.

"But if you'll just stay with us until I can get a
summer job and figure out what I'm going to do about
school . . ." Joe said tentatively.

"I be here," said Horace.

Joe, young and sad and newly bereaved, let himself

57

lean for a moment against the solid bulk of his black friend.

"Oh, Horace," he said, "if only we had enough money . . ."

"Ain't enough money to buy family," Horace said, polishing a julep cup. "I be's family. I staying."

Between them they did it. I was in their house a few times and it was a mess. No part of the furnishings with which the parents had begun housekeeping was ever replaced. Curtains fell into tatters. The oriental rugs, punished by "boy-boisterous" traffic, were ragged. The silver, which once gleamed lustrously, was so dull that when Joe served up mint juleps by his father's recipe, he noted in sudden surprise that the old julep cups looked like pewter instead of silver.

The kitchen, although basically clean, was in complete disorder with pots and pans and dishes left where they happened to be handy for use. They apparently considered it a waste of time to put up groceries or to make up beds, and when a boy snagged his shirt or trousers, he either mended it himself or wore it that way.

But when Stevie was stricken with polio, Horace and Joe worked over him day and night, applying the constant succession of hot packs — a treatment which the Australian nurse, Sister Elizabeth Kenny, advocated and which was in general use at that time. They pulled him through with only a little crippling in his legs, and he eventually overcame that with the help of the therapy, which Joe and Horace learned and painstakingly taught the other boys to administer.

Joe was able to finish college, working at a series of

part-time jobs, because Horace had moved into the house and was there to look after his brothers full-time.

They were by no means model boys, those brothers. Sometimes they played hooky from school. Occasionally one of them failed a subject and had to take it over. In a Roman Catholic family, it was unthinkable that they would miss mass, but Ed, at the age of twelve, decided to depart the church. He could no longer, he said loftily, put up with the disciplines of the church.

None too devout themselves, his older brothers didn't worry about Ed's soul but they were concerned about Joe's reaction. Having one of the young ones leave the church would be a major concern to him. So they tried to prevail upon Ed to stick it out, at least until Joe came home from the university. Ed pretended to accede, setting out for the cathedral with them. But after they were safely settled in their pews, he took off for the drugstore, where he read comic books and drank cherry smashes until the mass ended.

Horace, at home cooking Sunday dinner, heard from his friend, the drugstore delivery boy, that Ed was truant from church. The next Sunday, dressed in the blue serge suit he reserved for his own African Methodist Episcopal church service, Horace announced that he had decided to go to the Catholic church. With the dignified, dark-suited, gray-haired old black man beside him, Ed didn't have the nerve to detour by the drugstore.

They went to church, Horace and the five brothers, and entered the door side by side. In that color-conscious day, Horace took a seat on the back row, but his eyes were on his boys, and he patiently waited out the mass he didn't understand or particularly like. He went every Sunday until Joe came home and took over.

His own minister chided Horace about his absence from their church once, but I heard that Horace silenced him by saying simply: "Reverunt, I got my own lambs to shepherd."

Shepherd them he did. Once he showed up in juvenile court because Chuck had been seen smoking cigarettes with a group of boys back of a garage which was subsequently burned down. The fire marshal suspected them all. Joe was away and Horace called the family lawyer, who laughed and said it was nothing to worry about. He'd put in a call to somebody who could take care of it. To be sure, Horace thought he'd better try to take care of it himself. He again donned his Sunday suit and walked beside his boy to face the judge.

Chuck was terrified and his voice cracked a little as he swore that he was not present the day the garage burned and had nothing to do with setting it.

"That's right, sir," Horace said. "This boy not even there."

Expecting the old man to provide an alibi for the boy, the judge said, "And how do you know he wasn't there?"

"He *say* so," said Horace simply but with such conviction, such confidence it left no room for doubt.

The charge against Chuck was dismissed.

Chuck always said he couldn't have lied to Horace after that, even if he wanted to.

Joe was graduated from college and came home and

got a full-time job and, with all of them working part-time as they could, each of his brothers made it through the university. Joe was a handsome young man and he thought of getting married more than once, but somehow it never panned out. I often wondered if the girls he had in mind had taken a look at the old house and the big family who inhabited it and decided they weren't up to such mass mothering. Joe never married and neither did Horace.

The others did and moved into homes of their own, returning to the old house, where Joe and Horace batched, on holidays and vacations. I heard that their children called both Horace and Joe "uncle" and enjoyed visiting them. The last time I passed that way, the house had been torn down to make way for apartments, and I heard that both Joe and Horace were dead.

They were buried in different cemeteries and people who knew them well said it was a shame.

"They should have been buried side by side," a friend said, "with a joint tombstone reading, 'Their children rise up and call them blessed.'"

Chapter 7

ALL MOTHERS HAVE troubles and occasional crises, but few — particularly the loving, striving, dedicated ones — have to worry about being evicted, protested against and investigated. Few are publicly reprimanded for inadequate bookkeeping, too infrequent fire drills and maintaining a psychological atmosphere that is "counter-productive to learning." It would come as a shock to most mothers to look out on a band of marchers carrying placards proclaiming that "LOVE IS NOT ENOUGH."

Mae Hawkins thought love — love and food — might be enough when she saw her first new babies suffering from birth defects. She was a young student nurse at the University Hospital in Augusta, Georgia, and, looking for a shortcut back to her dormitory, she wandered for the first time into a room with six brain-damaged infants.

"I went on duty with them that night," she recalled half a century later. "They needed somebody and I've loved all I've ever seen since."

When she finished her nurses' training, Mae married Stacy Smith and moved to Atlanta, where she launched her nursing career and he entered the insurance business. They began what they hoped would be a big family with adoption of a little baby boy they named Stacy, Jr.

Ironically, the son they adored suffered brain damage following encephalitis (sleeping sickness) when he was three years old. The young mother promptly gave up her nursing career to stay at home with him. One summer she was asked to keep four normal children while their parents went on vacation, and she surprised herself at how much she enjoyed having them around.

Then someone brought her a newborn infant and she immediately fell in love with him, not knowing for weeks that he was blind and had massive brain damage.

"I don't know if his parents knew," she said. "They never came back."

So began the "family" which was to number more than a thousand defective and retarded children in the next fifty years.

"I think God let Stacy, Jr., live so I might do this," she said. "I took these children because I knew the heartbreak their parents went through."

Mae Smith never intended to run an institution. She hated the idea. She simply wanted a home as big as her heart — one that would accommodate the children who needed her, with plenty of time for rocking and hugging, for little songs and prayers and warmth and nourishing food. Her husband Stacy might have been dismayed at first by her preoccupation with other people's children, many of them very little ones who were destined to die early and would break her heart. He might reasonably have railed out that the neat pretty little house he could provide for his own family wasn't big enough to accommodate dozens of little strangers and, indeed, would be publicly enounced as "inadequate," even after new rooms were tacked on and plumbing and heating were extended. But according to his wife, he was with her every step of the way.

"He was a good man," she told me after his death in 1978. "You know, you can live with a man a hundred years and not know all the good he does. He was such a help to me in making it a home — a real home — for all my children. He used to go at night and talk to them and sit by them and have prayer with them."

Even after their "family" grew so big they had to hire a daytime staff of workers, the Smiths were alone with their little charges at night. They slept fully clothed and took turns getting up every two hours to check on the sleeping children. They share with most parents horror at the idea a little one might awaken in the night and cry out in loneliness and fear. And the thought that a child could die alone with no loved one to smooth its brow or hold its hand haunted both Mae and Stacy so that they frequently sat up all night beside a crib at home or in a hospital to face death with a baby.

There were few facilities for children suffering from birth defects when the Smiths started, and their home became the only hope of many parents, the only refuge for many children. At times they had as many as fifty-two children under their roof. Some of them were the children of well-to-do parents who could afford to pay. Some were the children of parents who could pay a little and many who could pay nothing.

"It doesn't matter," Mrs. Smith said. "I'll never let lack of money keep me from taking a baby. God will provide."

And God or His minions on earth — Sunday school classes and other church groups, civic clubs and private citizens — did provide a great deal. Volunteers came to help with cleaning and cooking and nursing. When crowding became a real problem, builders came and helped tack on a new room. Then the crisis of highway expansion struck.

Interstate 485 and the Stone Mountain freeway, projected highways which were to keep Atlantans in turmoil for many years, were routed through the Little Five Points neighborhood where the Smiths lived, and their house was condemned.

The urgency of the situation struck a DeKalb civic club that had helped the Smiths in the past, and the members, in an abundance of goodwill and enthusiasm, decided to make a new home their project.

Mrs. Smith was overwhelmed with gratitude. Then, as the fund raising moved apace, she began to have doubts. If these good men built a home for her children, there would be inevitable strings attached.

They had already formed a tax-exempt corporation and invited her to be on the board of directors. They had set $100,000 as their goal for the new "institute" and were already forseeing the day when Mrs. Smith, then seventy-three years old, would be "unable to carry on her work."

All of this began to worry Mrs. Smith, particularly that word "institute." It didn't sound like a home. She appreciated what the young men were doing, but she could see that her role, if any, would be to "sit in an office behind a desk," which she thought a poor second to "being with my babies."

She turned down the money. Regretfully, gratefully, she told the good-hearted donors, "No, thank you."

And with what money she could get together, she bought a house on Flat Shoals Avenue and enlisted the help of friends in getting it in order. At one time, there were thirty volunteer bricklayers on the lot, rushing to get an annex ready by Christmas.

Once in the new home, the Smith brood seemed to be flourishing. Honors came from many places for Mrs. Smith. The group of business and civic leaders who for thirty years had selected and honored outstanding women were ending the program, but they selected her to be the final recipient of their top honor — 1972 Woman of the Year. Her husband Stacy and three of their children, two little boys in wheelchairs and a little girl named Sarah, went along to the gala banquet in the Marriott hotel ballroom and broke into cheers when "Mama" was named THE Woman of the Year over four other WOTYs selected as outstanding in their individual fields.

With the expansion of the home and personal honors, however, came more trouble.

A discharged employee complained and the Atlanta Association for Retarded Citizens went forth to look over the Smith home and came back with a report criticizing overcrowded conditions, "improper" methods of restraining children in the grips of spasms and insufficient staff.

The State Department of Human Resources was asked to deny the home a license. Weary and troubled, Mae Smith saw a dozen of her children moved to other places, mostly state centers for evaluation. She knew the needs and the weaknesses in her house better than anybody else, but she had never been able to turn down a helpless child.

Her defenders were plentiful and vocal. Many were men and women whose brain-damaged children had been in her care for years. One woman physician wrote a particularly eloquent letter to the newspaper. She applauded any "technical improvements" the Department of Human Resources might effect, but she warned that they could not equal Mae's "magnificent contribution" in the peace and contentment she gave to her children and the tenderness they found in her home — "that alone their only haven of survival."

"I speak of this with feeling," she concluded, "because I have a mongoloid son who has received as near perfect care as could be given from Mrs. Smith for fifteen years."

T. M. (Jim) Parham, DHR commissioner, heard the complaints, received protesting groups with their placards and agreed to send out inspectors. But he couldn't help remarking that there was a tinge of self-righteousness in those late-day critics, many of whom were not even born forty-five years before when Mae Smith offered the only refuge for brain-damaged babies.

"We will investigate," he said, "but it will be like investigating an angel."

That crisis passed. A new license was granted along with a list of things to be done. Mrs. Smith accepted them and promised to "get right" with her critics. Posting menus and keeping better records weren't exactly high on her list of things essential to the well-being of her little ones, but she would do them.

The population of her home had thinned. Babies were being taken elsewhere. There were new regional retardation centers now. But she went cheerfully about making a home for those who were left to her when trouble struck again. She was on her way home from the grocery store with some special things for a birthday celebration for Joey, a retarded boy who had been with her most of his twelve years. Her car was hit by another car and, as she described it, "I was broken all over — so bad I should have died, but I guess the good Lord still has something for me to do."

Stacy, who had been ill for months, died shortly thereafter. Their son, then in his late forties, had to be moved to a state retardation center. Grieving for both of them, Mae went to her husband's funeral in a wheelchair.

Both losses haunted her still as she approached her ninetieth birthday. She grieved for her husband and she urged friends to go and see Stacy, Jr.

"He won't know it, but I will and I appreciate it," she said.

But most desperately she missed the little ones — "my other children."

"I hope and pray they are being looked after," she

69

said, and then her still-bright blue eyes filled with laughter at her own solemnity.

"You know how it is with Mama," she said. "She will go to her grave worrying that they might kick the cover off on a cold night or wake up lonely and scared."

Chapter 8

THE TROUBLE WITH being a mother is that there are no really trustworthy rules. Nearly any other form of endeavor has a reliable set of thou-shalts and thou-shalt-nots to guide the timid and bolster the fearful. Bachelors and old maids can tell you what to do when your children are small and grandmothers can tell you what you *should* have done when it's too late and they are already in jail, a mental institution or a fetid hippy haven somewhere.

But as you go along you founder on the shoals of conflicting advice from all the experts and harsh refutals of all the honored old homelies.

Once I covered a series of statewide meetings on juvenile delinquency. A legislative committee went from county seat to county seat, hearing anybody who wanted to be heard.

The ministers came out and said more attention to churches would save youth. A boy in Sunday school was a safe boy, etc.

The Boy Scouts and Girl Scouts said more public support of their programs would turn the tide in the generation's march toward perdition.

The recreation people said youth centers and playgrounds were the answer.

And through it all, over and over again, they all sounded the old refrain: "Broken homes, broken homes, broken homes. . . ."

Knowing something about broken homes I took that personally and went to the library and looked up a few great Americans. Five out of six were products of broken homes. About that time an Eagle Scout, active in church and Sunday school and the best all-round boy at the local youth center, went home and blew out the brains of both his parents and two sets of grandparents — demolishing with both barrels the legislative committee's best hope for a sure-fire formula.

Everybody knows at least one story about a heart-of-gold prostitute who has reared a child to be a statesman or a philanthropist or an ornament to medicine, the law or society in general. Sometimes orphans, school dropouts and delinquents make it. (Benjamin Franklin had but two years' schooling and was a runaway at seventeen.)

The discouraging thing is how often children will take a mother's good example and turn it on her. Recently, a young minister, showing me around Break Through House, a haven for young women who want to kick lives of prostitution, alcoholism or dope addiction, confided that nearly all of them came from deeply pious homes, where they were made to go to Sunday school and church regularly.

I had a momentary picture of a determinedly good mother starching and ironing clothes and turning out early on an otherwise sleepable Sabbath morn to "bring up a child in the way he should go" on the biblical promise that "when he is old he will not depart from it."

Sometimes their mother's example fills children with a fierce and perverse desire to be different.

My friend Marge used to alternately charm and alarm her friends with her child-rearing methods. Beautiful, funny, volatile and generous beyond all reason, she came from a college professor's family to which she, as they say nowadays, overreacted.

In the midst of a family of Phi Beta Kappas and Ph.D.s she delighted in bragging that she had made it through college without reading a book. She found her children's interest in books acceptable because it kept them quiet and from underfoot. But her husband's desire to read the evening paper or dip into the *Reader's Digest* struck her as a weakness comparable to alcoholism.

"He *reads*, you know," she used to whisper to friends in his presence.

Once, with the knowledge of all their four children, she undertook to break him of this execrable habit.

"He was reading the paper," she related, "and I wanted to talk. I tried to get his attention two or three times but he kept on reading. So I thought I'd call up somebody. Then I thought, 'They're probably reading, too.' I had a terrible mental picture of everybody in the whole world reading."

Finally, having seen the play *Harvey*, with a great

unseen, imaginary rabbit, she decided to make up a male companion who "can neither read nor write — has eyes and ears only for me." She called him Dream Man, soon to be shortened to D.M., and she would sit on the sofa across from where her husband sat to read and carry on imaginary conversations with D.M. If her husband looked up from his paper she would smile and say, "That's all right, dear. I'm with *him*."

"It hasn't exactly broken Husband of the reading habit," she later crowed to me, "But he doesn't *enjoy* it the way he used to!"

Every one of this woman's children got through college with honors and two or three went on to do graduate work. For some reason, her husband continues to adore her.

Homemaking was not an art that interested her particularly. If her husband planted a little vegetable garden she would give the produce away before he could harvest it. Meals from her kitchen were more likely to be thrifty than tasty. I remember seeing her chase down one of her young ones (the one, it developed later, with the nervous stomach), hold her and pour sauerkraut juice down her because it had been a bargain at the grocery store and she had bought a big supply of it. She bought their clothes at the church thrift shop, not because she needed to but because she wanted to help the church and hated the waste of new clothes. And although she loved pretty furniture and enjoyed a certain success as an antiques dealer she didn't spend any time arranging or keeping her house.

"Just put up a ladder in the living room," she told me

once. "It looks like you're moving, remodeling or doing heavy housecleaning. With a ladder up in the living room anything goes!"

At least one of her daughters worked as a mother's helper to learn gourmet cooking in France and never sits down to dinner without flowers and candles on the table, the linen immaculate, the silver gleaming and a precisely perfect wine cooling nearby.

Naturally beautiful with a great mop of tawny hair and flawless teeth which she shows frequently and totally in raucous, full-throated laughter, Marge has absolutely no interest in her appearance. Occasionally, when their children were young, her husband would look at her in church and realize that, lovely as she was, she didn't look like other women. Her dress, a little something she picked up at the thrift house, was losing its hem or had lost its buttons. And her hat — could that be a diaper she had coiled around her head? It was and what's more, the day before she had worn it to a tea.

A conventional man by nature, he would haul her off to town and personally supervise the fitting and purchase of a new outfit.

"Husband saw me through my ordeal," she would report, smiling on him dreamily.

One of her daughters is a couturière-type dressmaker who designs and makes every stitch of her own faultlessly chic wardrobe.

The moral of this, if any, is that mothers sometimes succeed without really trying.

One of the most revered women I know about, adored by her children and a legend to her grandchildren, was a good cook, but when her children were small and their father, a ship's captain, was away at sea she frequently hitched up the buggy and went off to visit the sick — or just visit — leaving her young to fend for themselves. They are all enormously self-reliant people and practically celebrated cooks.

She never heard of Philip Wylie's "momism" or the menace of possessive mothers and she jealously forbade her youngest son to leave her side and get married. When he did, with fear and trepidation, the bride he brought home was crazy about her.

He used to tell how his mother made courting difficult. When she ironed him a shirt she would press only the collar and the cuffs and a skinny strip down the front. If he pleaded with her to do it up properly, she would fling the shirt at him and say cheerfully, "Here. It won't show. You won't be taking off your coat anyhow."

Always speak the truth to children, mothers are told and I believe it. My own mother reared me on whoppers, but when I found out about the rule I tried to obey it. As a result my children grew up thinking their grandmother was a great deal more interesting than their stodgy mother.

Once when they were small they ran into her house, big-eyed and breathless over the "Wanted" posters they had been reading at the post office. They described a sinister red-headed bandit and Muv, shivering with excitement too, steered them up the road to where one of her ultrarespectable neighbors was peacefully plowing his corn. All afternoon my children wriggled on their bellies down freshly plowed furrows, keeping an eye on what they thought was a desperado.

It made the grownups' visit back at the house more serene, but was it right?

On another occasion I heard them ask Muv to tell them about her wedding. I had seen photographs and I knew that she was married quietly in an office or a study and wore a suit. The account she gave the children was a Cecil B. de Mille spectacle with two dozen long-stemmed bridesmaids, stained glass windows, church bells ringing, a mighty organ pealing, and her descending and ascending a splendid curving staircase pulling a train a quarter of a mile long.

"Who caught your bridal bouquet, Muv?" asked one of the little girls breathlessly.

"Why, your mother, of course!" she told them.

It seemed to me high time to interrupt and I did.

"Don't tell them that!" I cried. "They'll *believe* it!"

"Pooh," said Muv. "I wouldn't have literal-minded grandchildren."

It turned out that she didn't have literal-minded grandchildren and for the life of me I don't know if that's cause and effect.

Neither do I know what makes a woman a good mother. My research leads me to believe that being herself, truly herself, hanging on to her individuality in the face of current mores to the contrary, has never diminished a woman's achievement as a mother. Beyond that, the single gift all mothers have in common is that they love.

Chapter 9

MY OWN MOTHER, Muv, died a few years after this book was first published in 1970. In a story in the *Constitution* about her death, Harold Martin, my long-time friend and office roommate, was quoted as calling her "merry and wise."

If, given her choice of adjectives, as none of us can be when our obituaries are written, Muv might have chosen something else. She admired that "virtuous woman" in Proverbs and would have surely opted for that. I don't know why it doesn't seem to me to fit, for she certainly couldn't be called unvirtuous.

She had a great respect for learning and would have been wistfully aware that she wasn't entitled to be called "learned" or "scholarly," although she was what may even be better — an undaunted, unflagging learner.

She might have liked to go into that other world called "sweet," although I can't believe it. She and I have shared an antipathy to "sweet" people, an ancient conviction that the sugar-mouthed is not for real, that honeyed words and hypocrisy go together. Still, if she ever fell into the company of a bonafide, undiluted "sweet" woman, Muv was awed and impressed into taking on the coloration and acting sweet herself. It made me very nervous when I was a child. I figured that she was up to something. My children felt the same way. We had ample reason.

Once when we had house guests and I was needed to help out in the kitchen, I overslept and was awakened by Muv's dulcet call from the yard outside the sleeping porch.

"Open the door, sweetie," she wheedled softly. Befuddled by sleep, I stumbled to the door, all unsuspecting, and unlatched the screen.

Muv was on me in an instant, brandishing the big butcher knife she'd been using to slice bacon.

"What do you mean laying up in the bed all day?" she snarled. "I'll teach you . . . !"

"Don't kill me, Muv! Don't kill me!" I begged, looking at the knife.

She saw it too and collapsed in laughter.

She hadn't meant to scare me *that* much. If it had been necessary, I always felt, she would have used it, but she hadn't ever even spanked me. I scared easy.

The words, "Come here, sweetie," can send my children charging in the other direction. They remember well the day Muv found that Mary had failed to put out her kitten at night. She collected the evidence on a shovel and summoned Mary in from play with a persuasive, beguiling, "Come here, sweetie!"

The contents of the shovel and the little girl landed

at the same place at the same time — a memorable meeting. Mary never again deprived a cat of access to toilet facilities.

Sweet? No, Muv wouldn't make it.

Merry and wise?

Merry, surely. She loved to laugh. She was a great mimic, and when she found that her grandchildren mimicked her, she was their best audience. Once she caught her grandson, Jimmy, portraying her in her role of Sunday school superintendent. He put on her Sunday hat, hooked her bag over his arm and talked in an unbelievably prissy, officious tone. She thought it was a riot and made him perform again and again. She even thought it was funny when he "did" me. ("Look, here's Mama running late for work!") But my sense of humor wasn't as sturdy as hers. It wilted when I was the object of their laughter.

She was a gifted storyteller and the world's best listener. If I went to a party, she waited up to get a rundown on who was there and how they behaved. For years after I went to a country candy pull given by my classmate in the fourth grade, she made me do the excessively polite but tongue-tied fellow who sought out all the grown girls in the crowd and told them he was "nappy to neet noo."

She scoffed at people who grieved audibly or suffered ostentatiously. "Putting on airs," she called it. And when she heard that a cousin of hers had lamented loudly and threatened to jump when they filled her brother's grave, she ridiculed the cousin to her face, condemning her to a future of dull and phlegmatic mourning.

She aimed to be a pillar of rectitude. I know that. But she was friends with her town's only known prostitute. She picked up a pistol and brandished it in the face of a wife-beater. (I'm not even sure it wasn't loaded. She occasionally practiced target shooting.) One summer night when we sat under her pecan tree in the back-yard drinking a beer, one of her church friends came to visit and she tried to fob the beer off as iced tea.

Sweetly, graciously, she said, "Won't you have some of this tea, Sarah?"

I was shocked two ways: One, that she thought Sarah was fooled, and two, that she would do what she taught me not to do — act a lie.

She dismissed her deceit lightly on the ground that it was motivated by her vast respect for Sarah's well-known aversion to spirits.

I had trouble straightening out that moral issue, just as I had trouble with her tenets against Sunday work. It was a violation of the Sabbath and, besides that, plain bad management to wash clothes or paint a wall or cut grass on Sunday, she decreed. When I caught her doing some of these things, she said loftily, "The better the day, the better the deed."

She loved to sing, to dance, to picnic, to travel — anywhere, anytime. An omnivorous reader, she had very little formal education, and when the principal of the school in her town asked her to teach, she was miserable about turning him down.

"I'm not *educated*!" she wailed.

"Why, you're one of the best educated women I know," he said. "You don't have a degree?"

She didn't have, so she packed up her nice voile

dresses and her arch support shoes and went to college. I have some of the silver she bought with her earnings, and I talked to a man recently who said she was the best teacher he ever had.

As for wisdom, bits and pieces of her teachings come back to me now and then. She believed firmly that as you sow so shall you reap, that good must be returned for evil, that you only have what you give away. Clichés perhaps, but not to her. They were lively, provable truths, and when she violated one of them, she suffered. And yet she could hold a grudge against anyone who hurt those she loved, and I know, as certainly as the sun brings morning, that she was capable of killing to protect her family.

Wisdom, I sometimes think, was in her bones, a born sapience that made her love life and laughter and make allowances for pain and grief.

Once I asked a woman how long after her death you go on thinking about your mother and missing her. "I don't know," she said. "Mine has been gone for twenty-five years and I think of her every day."

The answer, I suppose, is forever.